Johanna Ries was born in Marl, Germany. While she was still a child, she discovered the joys of painting and writing stories. In 2015, she began her studies in illustration at the Münster School of Design, specializing in illustrating both fiction and nonfiction. She graduated in July 2018, with *The Speckled Feather* as part of her final examination.

THE SPECKLED FEATHER

by Johanna Ries

Translated by David Henry Wilson

North South

Elephants live in the savanna. They are so big and gray that you can see them from miles away. But if you dare to go closer, you will realize that someone else is there too....

On the back of the elephant sit birds. High above the savanna grass they are safe from predators. What's more, they can see quite a distance from the elephant's back.

Once upon a time there were three snow-white birds that lived on the back of an elephant. He called them

ADE, EMEM, and NURU.

Ade was the quickest of the three, Emem liked to climb all over the elephant's trunk, and Nuru found the fattest insects in the gray folds of the elephant's skin. There were never any quarrels on the elephant's back.

One day a dusty wind blew through the savanna.

A particularly strong gust carried a BRIGHT SPECKLED FEATHER over the grass and as far as the herd of elephants . . .

...where Ade, the fastest of the three birds, grabbed it out of the air.

"What a gorgeous speckled feather!" said the delighted Ade, and he stuck the feather into his own plumage. Then he flapped his wings and flew far away from his friends, sat on the elephant's head, and poked his tongue out at the others.

"IT'S MY SPECKLED FEATHER!" he crowed.

"I'm the first bird on this elephant and so the feather belongs to me!"

Around midday it got so hot in the savanna that the elephant stopped at a water hole. Ade leaned quite a long way forward to see whether he and his feather were reflected in the water.

"Look how handsome I am!" he boasted. "I'm the most beautiful bird in the whole savanna!"

"I want a speckled feather too!" whined Nuru from his place on the elephant's behind.

"Me too!" moaned Emem. "And in any case it would look much better on me than on Ade!"

"If we steal the feather, you and I can share it," suggested Nuru.

Emem thought for a moment and then he nodded. In fact, he wanted the feather all to himself, but he kept quiet about that.

Very softly the two birds hopped toward Ade....

But then ...

"THIEVES!" screeched Ade. "YOU WANT TO STEAL MY FEATHER!"

While the birds were quarreling,
the elephant raised his trunk . . . and huffed and puffed
and blew and blasted
the birds down off his back.

"ENOUGH!"

The elephant stamped his foot angrily. "The three of you will get rid of this feather and will make friends! I won't let you sit on my back again until you do!"

Emem and Nuru nervously stretched their necks up over
the grass, but the backs of all the other elephants were occupied.
"Throw the speckled feather away!" begged Nuru. "Then we
can sit on our elephant again!"
But Ade refused to give in.

"MY FEATHER STAYS WITH ME."

Night began to fall around the elephants. The three
quarreling birds could be heard all over the savanna.
Lured by the noise, something approached in the dark.

The shadow came ever closer through the tall grass; but Ade, Emem, and Nuru never noticed the glowing yellow eyes. On the contrary, the squabble became louder and louder.

THEN SUDDENLY . . .

A large, gray, powerful something

The elephant swung his trunk
and hurled the wild dog away in a high arc.
And the speckled feather went whirling through the air as well. . . .

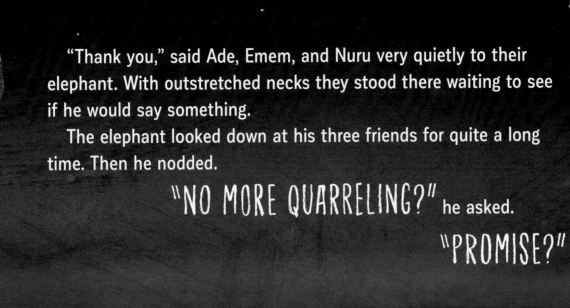

"Thank you," said Ade, Emem, and Nuru very quietly to their elephant. With outstretched necks they stood there waiting to see if he would say something.

The elephant looked down at his three friends for quite a long time. Then he nodded.

"NO MORE QUARRELING?" he asked.

"PROMISE?"